The Little Mermaid

Commemorative Edition

The Little Mermaid

by Hans Christian Andersen

Commemorative Edition
on the
100 Year Anniversary
of
The Little Mermaid Statue

The Little Mermaid
Commemorative Edition

Cover by: Philip M. Jepsen
Cover photo by: James Bilbrey

Original Title: **Den Lille Havfrue**

Author: **Hans Christian Andersen**

First Edition: **1837**

English Translation by Ragnhild Munck (2013)
Compilation and Editing by Philip Jepsen

ISBN-13: 978-0-9889454-0-1

Book Website: www.mermaidsofearth.com/tlm2013
Email: philip@mermaidsofearth.com

Give feedback on the book at: philip@mermaidsofearth.com

Printed in U.S.A

Preface

The fairy tale "The Little Mermaid" by Hans Christian Andersen is

known throughout the world. This is of course partly because Disney has made it popular with its movie adaptation released in 1989, but it was a very famous story even before Disney made its film version, and indeed the first translation into English was done in 1872 by Henry H.B. Paull.

Hans Christian Andersen

The first of the many statues of *The Little Mermaid* was made in 1913, and it has been a symbol of Copenhagen and Denmark for a hundred years now.

This book is a modern translation into English from the original Danish fairy tale by Hans Christian Andersen, as originally published in 1837.

The Hans Christian Andersen story is quite different from the Disney version, and it is well worth reading the original.

The fairy tale has been performed many times at the Royal Danish Ballet in Copenhagen. It was here that the ballet performance was seen by Danish brewer, art collector and philanthropist Carl Jacobsen, son of J. C. Jacobsen, who founded the brewery Carlsberg and named it after him. Carl was so taken by the ballet that he commissioned the famous statue in Copenhagen in 1909. Sculptor Edvard Eriksen

Carl Jacobsen

finished the sculpture in 1913, using his wife Eline Eriksen as the model

for the statue. It was unveiled in its present location in the beautiful Langelinie park by the Copenhagen Harbor on August 23rd, 1913.

Eline Eriksen   Edvard Eriksen

2013 thus marks the 100 Year Anniversary of this famous statue, which has been copied around the world, and even traveled to China for a short time in 2010 for the Shanghai World Expo.

This edition of the story commemorates the centennial of Edvard Eriksen's mermaid statue, and is illustrated with photos of the statue and some of its replicas around the world. Also included are four illustrations by Vilhelm Pedersen for this story.

Vilhelm Pedersen

Pedersen's illustrations were the first illustrations of Hans Christian Andersen's stories, produced for an 1849 book of collected works.

My sincere appreciation and thanks to all those who assisted in making this work possible. In particular I want to thank my mother Ragnhild for her translation from the original Danish fairy tale and for her inspiration, my wife Pamela for her patience and support, editing, proofreading and her many wonderful suggestions.

Lastly, I want to thank the hundreds of artists who have created so many fabulous mermaid statues all over the world, as shown on *mermaidsofearth.com*.

I hope you enjoy the story, the photos and the illustrations.

Philip

2

For My Sister

Maria Patricia Munck

She adored Hans Christian Andersen's
fairy tales, and would have
thoroughly enjoyed
this book.

Original Illustration by Vilhelm Petersen, 1849

The Little Mermaid

Far out at sea the water is as blue as the loveliest cornflower and as clear as the purest of crystal, and very, very deep - deeper than any anchor can reach. Many church steeples would have to be placed on top of each other to reach from the bottom to the surface. Down there is where the Sea King and his people live.

Don't think that the bottom is just plain white sand. No indeed, the most wonderful trees and plants grow there, with stalks and leaves so delicate that the slightest movement in the water causes them to bend and dance as if they were alive. All the fish, both small and big, weave amongst the branches as do birds in the air up here. At the very deepest place the King of the Sea has his castle. Its walls are made of coral and its long pointed windows are of the clearest amber. The roof is made of cockleshells which open and close as the water flows. It looks very beautiful, as in each cockleshell is a radiant pearl - each pearl of such radiance that it would look brilliant in the crown or tiara of a queen.

The Sea King who lives there had been a widower for many years. His aging mother who kept house for him was a wise woman, but

The original statue of The Little Mermaid, by Edvard Eriksen, unveiled on August 23, 1913. Except for a trip to China in 2010, the statue has remained here at the beautiful Langelinie Park in the Copenhagen Harbor area since 1913. Photo © by James Bilbrey. The Little Mermaid is visited by millions and is a symbol of Copenhagen and of Denmark. Website at http://goo.gl/4AJEL

exceedingly proud of her high birth, on which account she wore 12 oysters on her tail, while others of nobility were allowed only 6 oysters each. She did, however, deserve a lot of praise, especially because she was so very fond of the small mermaids, her son's daughters. There were 6 lovely children, but the youngest was the loveliest of all. Her skin was as clear and delicate as a rose petal, her eyes as blue as the deepest lake. But like all the others she had no feet. Her body ended in a fish tail.

All day long they would play down in the castle, in the great halls where live flowers grew out of the walls. The large amber windows were kept open and the fish would swim in, just as up here the swallows fly in to our houses when we open our windows. The fish would swim straight up to the little princesses and eat out of their hands and let themselves be stroked.

Around the castle was a large garden with bright red and dark blue trees. The fruits shone like gold and the flowers like a burning fire among the constantly moving stalks and leaves. The ground was of the finest sand, except it was as blue as a flame of sulphur. Over everything there was an exquisite blue hue. You could almost believe you were high up in the air and saw heaven both above and beneath you, rather than being at the bottom of the sea. When the sea was calm it was possible to see the sun, which looked like a purple flower from which all the light came streaming out.

Each of the little princesses had her own spot in the garden where she could dig and plant just as she fancied; one made her plot look like the shape of a whale, another wanted hers to look like a mermaid. The youngest of them made her garden round like the sun and had only flowers in it which looked like little red suns. She was a strange child, quiet and thoughtful. The other sisters decorated their gardens with the strangest things collected from the wrecks of ships, but she had just the rose colored flowers and a beautiful marble

Original Illustration by Vilhelm Petersen, 1849

statue of a lovely boy. It was carved out of a clear white stone and had fallen to the bottom of the sea from a shipwreck. Next to the statue she planted a rose colored weeping willow, which grew marvelously. It spread its fresh branches over the statue and down towards the sand where the shadows turned violet and danced with the branches. It looked as if the top of the tree and its roots played a kissing game.

More than anything she wanted to hear about the human world above. The old grandmother had to tell her everything she knew about ships and cities, humans and animals. She was especially intrigued to learn that up there the flowers gave off delicious fragrances, so unlike flowers at the bottom of the sea, and that the forests were green, and that the fish seen among the branches could sing so loud and beautiful that it was a joy to hear. The grandmother called the little birds fishes to ensure the little mermaids would understand her, as they had never seen a bird.

"When you turn fifteen," said the grandmother, "you will be allowed to rise to the surface of the sea and to sit on the rocks in the moonlight and watch the large ships that sail by and perhaps see the forests and cities."

The following year one of the sisters was about to turn fifteen, but the other five sisters – well, each was a year younger than the next one, so it would be all of five years before the youngest was allowed up from the bottom of the sea to learn what our world looks like. Each promised to tell the others what she saw and liked the most on her first day at the surface, as their grandmother did not tell them enough. There was so much they wanted to know.

None of them longed more than the youngest, she who had the longest to wait and who was so quiet and thoughtful. Many an evening she stood at the open window and looked up through the blue water where the fish flipped their fins and tails. She could see the moon and the stars even though they only sent a pale light, but through the water they looked much larger than through our eyes. And when a large cloud passed under them she knew that it would be either a whale or a ship with many humans who probably could not imagine that a lovely mermaid was below them and stretched her white hands up toward the keel of the ship.

At last the eldest mermaid turned fifteen and dared approach the surface.

Replica of the statue of The Little Mermaid. This copy was placed at the Forest Lawn Cemetery in Glendale California by British actress Greer Garson in memory of her mother. Photo by © Doug Williams. Website at http://goo.gl/vnVx6

When she returned she had a hundred things to talk about, but the most beautiful, she said, was to lie in the moonlight on a sand dune in the calm sea, looking at the large city near the coast where lights blinked like a hundred stars, listening to the music and the rumblings of carriages and the voices of humans, seeing the many church steeples and hearing the merry pealing of bells. As she could not go up there amongst it all, she longed all the more for all these wonderful things.

Oh, how the youngest sister listened to these descriptions, and when later in the evening she was by the window looking up through the dark blue water, she thought of the big city and all the noise and commotion. And then she thought that maybe she could even make out the sound of the church bells ringing from where she was.

The following year the next sister was allowed to rise up through the water and swim where she wished. She emerged just as the sun went down and she found this to be the most beautiful. She said that the sky looked like gold and the clouds, well, their beauty she could not even describe. They had sailed above her, red and purple. But much faster than the clouds, a flock of swans flew like a long white veil across the water past the sun. She swam towards it, but it disappeared and the rosy hue faded on the sea and the clouds.

A year later the third sister went up. She was the most daring of them all, and she swam up a wide river running into the sea. She saw lovely green hills with beautiful vines and castles and farms among gorgeous forests. She had heard the birds sing and the sun had been so hot that she often had to dive under water to cool her burning face. In a small bay she saw a whole crowd of small human children. Quite naked, they were running around splashing in the water. She wanted to play with them, but they ran away quite frightened, and then a small black animal started barking fiercely at her, and she became so scared that she went to the open sea. But she could never forget the gorgeous forests, the green hills and the pretty children who could swim on the water even though they did not have fish tails.

The fourth sister was not so daring. She stayed out in the middle of the ocean and said that this was the best of all. She could see for miles around and the sky above was like a clear glass bowl. She had seen ships, but they had been so far away they looked like seagulls. The dolphins had made somersaults, and the big whales had sprayed water from their blow holes so that it looked like a hundred fountains in the sea.

Then it was the turn of the fifth sister, whose birthday was in the winter and therefore she saw what the others had missed the first time they went up. The sea looked so very green and large icebergs were drifting around. Each looked like a pearl and yet was larger than the church towers that humans built. They glittered like diamonds in the strangest formations. She had been sitting on one of the biggest of these, and when terrified sailors saw her there with her long hair flowing in the wind they steered around it. That night the sky was covered in clouds. There was thunder and lightning and the black waves heaved the large icebergs way up so they were lit up by the strong flashes of lightning. On all the ships she saw the sails were taken down by scared and terrified sailors, but she sat quite calm on her floating iceberg and saw the blue rays of lightning zig-zag down into the shining sea.

The first time any of the sisters emerged over the surface of the sea, they were delighted at the new and beautiful things they saw, but over time as they were now grownup girls and were allowed to go up whenever they wanted, the things above the sea became less interesting. They longed for home, and after about a month they said that down where they lived was the most beautiful and it was so nice to feel at home.

Many an evening the five sisters held hands as they came above the sea together. They had beautiful voices, lovelier than any human being, and when a storm was coming and they thought perhaps some ships might be wrecked they would swim in front of the ships and sing enchanting songs about how beautiful it was at the bottom of the sea

This half size replica of the statue of The Little Mermaid sits at Carlsberg Breweries in Copenhagen, Denmark. The original statue was commissioned by Carl Jacobsen of Carlsberg Breweries, and this smaller copy was installed at Carlberg Breweries in 1937. Photo © by David Barber. Website at http://goo.gl/625fX

and they asked the sailors not to be afraid to come down there. But the sailors did not understand the words and thought it was the wind. Also, they would never see the beauty below which the mermaids described, because humans would drown when the ship sank and they would be dead when they came to the Sea King's castle.

So when in the evenings her older sisters rose up high through the sea, arm in arm, the little youngest sister was left alone looking after them. And it was as if she wanted to cry, but mermaids have no tears, and therefore she suffered so much more.

"If only I were fifteen years old," she said, "I know that I will love the world up there and the people who build and live there."

At last she turned fifteen.

"Now we'll get you off our hands," said her grandmother, the old dowager queen. "Come here and let me dress you, just like I dressed your sisters." And she placed a wreath of white lilies on her hair. Every leaf in each flower was half a pearl. And the old lady fixed eight large oysters on the tail of the princess to show her nobility.

"It hurts," said the little mermaid.

"Well, we must suffer somewhat for the privilege," said the old grandmother.

Oh, how she would have preferred to shake off the entire splendor and do away with the heavy wreath; her red flowers from the garden suited her much better, but she did not dare to change.

"Good bye!" she said and as easy and light as a bubble she rose up through the waters.

The sun had just gone down as she lifted her head up above the surface of the sea, but all the clouds were still shining like roses and gold, and in the rose colored air the evening star shone clear and beautiful. The air was mild and fresh, the sea beautifully calm. She saw a large ship with three masts but only one sail up, as there was no wind. The seaman sat around in the ropes and yards of the topmast. There was music and song, and as the evening grew darker hundreds of colored lanterns were lit. It was as if the flag of every nation was seen in the air.

The little mermaid swam very close to a porthole, and every time the water carried her up she could look in through the bright windows and see many fancily clad humans standing there. The most handsome of them was the young prince with large dark eyes. He could hardly be more than 16 years old. It was his birthday and the festivities were for him. The seamen were dancing on the deck, and when the young prince stepped out, more than a hundred rockets were sent up in the air. They made the sky look like daytime and the little mermaid got such a scare that she dove under the surface. She soon emerged and it was as if all the stars in heaven descended upon her. Never before had she seen such fireworks. There were large pinwheels, glorious shining fish seemed to swim in the blue air, and everything was reflected back in the calm sea. The ship was lit up so every little rope was visible, as were the people. Oh, how handsome the young prince was, laughing and smiling and shaking hands with the people while the music was playing in the enchanted night.

It grew late, but the little mermaid could not take her eyes off the ship or the lovely prince. The colored lamps were turned off and the rockets no longer shot up in the air. The cannon ceased firing, but deep down in the sea there was a growling, buzzing sound. She sat in the water which lifted her up and down so she could look into the cabin. The ship started moving faster, as one sail after another was raised. The waves grew bigger and large clouds accumulated. Far away there was lightning. Oh, it was going to be a terrible storm, so the sailors took the sails down again.

The large ship was rolling and moved with great speed on the wild ocean. Waves rose like large, black mountains as if to cover the mast, but the ship dove like a swan down with the tall waves and up again on the towering waters. The little mermaid thought this was a thrilling ride, but the sailors did not appreciate it. The ship groaned and creaked in the joints, the heavy planks swelled out from the heavy push by the waves. Suddenly the mainmast broke as if it was a reed and the ship keeled over on its side while the water burst into the cabin. The little mermaid saw that the crew was in danger, and she herself had to be careful not to be hit by beams and debris from the ship.

This 4/5 size replica of the statue of The Little Mermaid, belonging to the heirs of sculptor Edvard Eriksen, was on loan to Tivoli Gardens in Copenhagen in 2010 while the original was in China at the Shanghai World Expo. Photo © by Benny Hansen. Website at http://goo.gl/kESLi

One moment it was so completely dark that she could not see anything, but then flashes of lightning made it so clear that she could see them all on the ship, each managing as best he could, except the prince. As the ship broke up further, she briefly saw him falling into the deep waves. At first she was very pleased, for now he would come down to be with her, but then she remembered that humans could not live in the sea and that he would be quite dead if he came to her father's castle. No, he must not die.

So she swam amongst the beams and planks that were floating in the sea, heedless of the danger that they might crush her. She dove deep under the surface and up again amongst the waves and at last reached the young prince who was fast losing the strength to keep swimming in the raging seas. His arms and legs were getting tired, the beautiful eyes closed, and he would have died if the little mermaid had not arrived. She kept his head above the water and they drifted wherever the waves carried them through the night.

In the morning the rough weather had passed, and nothing was left to be seen of the ship. The sun rose red and shining above the water and it was as if the prince's cheeks came alive, though his eyes were still closed. The mermaid kissed his forehead and brushed back his wet hair. She thought he resembled the marble statue she had in her little garden. She kissed him again and wished that he might live.

Ahead of her she now saw land, with tall, blue mountains capped with white snow. The sun reflecting off the snow made it seem as if the mountains were covered with swans. Near the coast there were lush, green forests and in front of these was a church or a monastery, she did not really know which, but it was some sort of building. There were citrus and orange trees in the garden and in front of the gate were tall palm trees. There was a little bay, where the water was calm, but very deep all the way to the rocks and there was fine white sand which formed the beach. To this place she swam with the handsome prince, and laid him on the powdery sand while being careful that his head was far from the water and in the sun.

This half size replica of the statue of The Little Mermaid was placed in the International Peace Gardens in Salt Lake City, Utah, in 1955, as Denmark's contribution to these gardens. Photo © by Nancy & Glen Carlson. Website at http://goo.gl/3CHKb

The bells started ringing in the large, white building and a group of young girls came walking down through the garden. The little mermaid swam out to hide behind some tall rocks rising out of the water. She covered her hair and neck with sea-foam, so no one could see her little face while she watched to see who would come to the poor prince.

It was not long before a young girl came very close. At first she seemed frightened, but only for a moment, then she gathered more people, and the mermaid saw how the prince came to life. He smiled at them all around him, but he did not smile in her direction - he could not know that she had saved him. She felt so sad at this, and when he was taken into the large building she dove in distress into the water and back to her father's castle.

She had always been a quiet and thoughtful child, now she became even more so. Her sisters asked her what she had seen on her first visit up there, but she would not tell.

Many an evening and morning she swam up to the place where she had left the prince. She saw the fruits ripen in the garden and being harvested. She saw the snow melt on the mountains, but she did not see the prince. Each time she returned home a little sadder. Her only consolation was to sit in her little garden and put her arms around the beautiful marble statue that looked like the prince. She no longer took care of her flowers, which grew into a wilderness, covering the paths and entangling the branches of the trees so it became quite dark and gloomy.

Finally she could not stand it any longer and confided in one of her sisters. Immediately all the other sisters were told, but no one else, except a few other mermaids, who told no one except a few close friends. One of them knew who the prince was. She too had seen the splendor on the ship, and she knew where he lived and where his kingdom was.

Come, little sister! The other princesses said, and with their arms around each other they rose in a long row up to the surface of the sea where they knew the prince had his castle.

It was built with glazed yellow stones and had long flights of marble stairs, one of which went all the way down to the sea. Magnificent golden domes rose above the roof and between columns placed all around the building were marble statues that seemed life-like and almost alive. Through the clear glass in the tall windows you could look into wonderful halls where costly silk drapes and tapestries hung. On the walls were lovely paintings which were a pleasure to look at. In the middle of the largest hall the splashing of a large fountain could be heard. The water shot up high towards the glass dome in the roof, where sunbeams hit the water and the lovely plants growing in the large basin.

Now she knew where he lived and many an evening and night she visited. She swam much closer to land than any of the others had ever dared, even all the way into the small channel under the gorgeous marble balcony that cast a shadow over the water. Here she sat and looked at the young prince who believed he was all alone in the bright moonlight.

Often she saw him sail in his magnificent boat with music and flying colors. She would peep out from between the green reeds, and if the wind lifted her long silvery veil and somebody saw it they probably thought it was a swan lifting its wings.

Many an evening when the fishermen were on the water with their lanterns she heard them relate many good things about the young prince and his actions, and it pleased her that she had saved his life when he was half dead and floundering on the waves. She remembered how his head had rested on her chest and with what passion she had kissed him. But he did not know this, and could not even dream about her.

More and more she became so fond of human beings that she wished she could rise up and walk amongst them in their world, which seemed so much larger than hers. They could fly across the sea in their ships and they could climb the high mountains over the clouds. The land they owned stretched with fields and forests longer than the eye could see. There was so much she wanted to know, but the sisters did not know the answers to everything, and so she asked the old grandmother. She knew about the world up there, which she quite properly called "The lands above the sea".

"Can the humans live forever if they do not drown," asked the little mermaid, "do they not die like we do in the sea?"

"Yes," said the old one, "they must also die, and their lifespan is shorter than ours. We can live three hundred years, but when we die we turn into foam on the water. We do not even have a grave here among our dear ones. We do not have immortal souls. We do not live again, but are instead like the green reeds - once cut down they cannot grow green again. But human beings have a soul which lives forever. It lives after the body has turned to dust, and then rises up through the clear air, up to all the shining stars. Just as we rise up to see the lands of humans, so they rise up to unknown beautiful places, those we shall never see."

"Why did we not get an immortal soul?" asked the little mermaid sadly. "I would give all my hundreds of years of life if I could become a human for just one day and later participate in the heavenly world."

"You should not think about things like that," said the old one, "we are much happier and fare better than the humans up there."

"So I must die and float like foam on the sea, and never hear the music of the waves or look upon the beautiful flowers and the red sun. Is there nothing I can do to win an immortal soul?"

"No," said the old woman, "only if a man loved you so much that you were dearer to him than his father and mother, and his thoughts and love was directed at you and he let the priest place his right hand

A slightly different version of the statue of The Little Mermaid, placed in 2010 in the Parque Europa just outside Madrid, Spain. Photo © by Andrés Moreno. Website at http://goo.gl/aNxfm

in yours with the promise that he would always be true to you, then his soul could flow into your body and you would participate in human happiness. He would give you his soul, yet also still have it. But this can never happen. What we find so beautiful here in the sea, your fish tail, they consider ugly up there on land. They do not know any better, they must have two clumsy sticks they call legs, in order to be beautiful."

The little mermaid drew a big sigh and looked sadly at her fish tail. "Let us have some fun," said the old grandmother, "let us hop and dance during the three hundred years we have to live in, which is really time enough - and after we can rest so much the better. Tonight we will have a royal ball."

There was more splendor than you would ever see on land. The walls and the loft in the great hall were made of thick, transparent

A local version of the statue of The Little Mermaid, in Kimballton Iowa. Kimballton and its neighboring town Elk Horn have a substantial Danish heritage, including The Little Mermaid and a large authentic Danish windmill. Photo © by Kevin Nelson. Website at http://goo.gl/0huni

crystal glass. There were several hundred enormous mussel shells, some rose colored, some green. They stood in rows on each side with a blue burning fire which lit up the entire hall and shone out through the walls, so that the sea outside was quite illuminated.

Untold numbers of fishes, large and small, swam past the crystal walls, some with brilliantly glowing purple scales, others with scales that seemed to shine like silver and gold. Down through the middle of the hall there was a swift current on which mermen and mermaids danced to their own delightful songs, in voices whose beauty no human voice possessed. The little mermaid sang with the most beautiful voice of them all and they applauded her performance. For a moment she felt joy in her heart for she knew that she had the most wonderful voice of all, on land and in the sea. But soon she again thought about the world above - she could not forget the handsome prince nor get over her sorrow at not having an immortal soul like he did. She quietly left her father's castle; away from the fun and music to sit alone, desolate in her little garden.

Suddenly, she heard the sound of a bugle right down through the water and she thought: "Now he must be sailing up there, he whom I cherish more than father and mother; he who is always in my thoughts and in whose hand I will place my life's happiness. I will venture anything to win him and an immortal soul. While my sisters are dancing merrily in my father's castle, I will go to the sea witch, whom I have always feared, but who perhaps can give counsel and help."

The little mermaid left her garden and headed towards the roaring maelstrom behind which lived the witch. She had never been that way before. There were no flowers and no seagrass, only the bare, grey sandy bottom stretching toward the maelstroms. They were like huge wheels spinning around, tearing everything in their way down into the depth of the sea. Through these roaring whirls she had to travel in order to reach the realms of the sea witch, and then for a long stretch there was no other way than over warm bubbling mire. The witch called it her peat bog. Behind this was her house, in the middle of a strange forest in which the trees and bushes were polyps, half animal, half plant. They looked like snakes with hundreds of heads, growing out of the ground. Their branches were long, slimy arms with fingers like supple worms, and they moved joint by joint from the roots to the end. Anything in the sea they could get hold of they would grasp and would never let go again.

The little mermaid stood still for a while before this vile forest, her heart beating fast with anxiety, almost making her turn back. But then she thought about the prince and the human soul she wanted and regained her courage. She tied her long flowing hair tight around her head so the

This interpretation of the statue of The Little Mermaid was given to the city of Pietra Neamt in Romania by Denmark's queen Margrethe while visiting in 2000. Website at http://goo.gl/Mas7l

polyps would not be able to grasp it, and folded her hands across her chest and darted forward as a fish through the water, between the ugly polyps stretching their slimy arms and fingers towards her. She saw how each of them had something they had caught, held by hundreds of little arms like strong iron bands. Humans beings who had perished at sea and had sunk down to the bottom were seen as white bony skeletons in the arms of the polyps. They held ships rudders, chests and skeletons of land animals. They also held a small mermaid they had caught and strangled, which to the little mermaid was the most horrible and shocking of all.

She then came to a large, slimy place in the forest, where big fat water snakes played around and showed their ugly white and yellow bellies. In the middle of this place was a house built of the bones of drowned sailors. Here the sea witch sat and let a toad eat out of her mouth, just like a human would let a canary bird eat sugar. She called the ugly, fat water snakes her little chickens and let them crawl around on her large spongy bosom.

"I know what you want," said the sea witch. "It is a stupid wish, but you shall have it your way, as it will bring you unhappiness, my lovely princess. You want to get rid of your fish tail and instead have two short stumps to walk on like the humans, so that the young prince will fall in love with you, and you can have him and an immortal soul." The sea witch laughed so loudly and nastily that the toad and the snakes fell to the ground and wriggled about. "You are just in time," said the witch, "for by tomorrow when the sun rises I would not be able to help you, and you would have to wait another year. I will make you a potion and before the sun is up you have to swim up to the land and sit on the shore and drink it. Then your tail will split and shrink into what the humans call their pretty legs. But it will hurt, feeling as if a sharp sword were going through you. All who see you will say that you are the most beautiful human child they have ever seen. You will keep your floating way of moving, and no dancing girl will be as graceful as you. But every step you take will feel as if you are stepping on a sharp knife that would make your blood flow. If you are ready to suffer all this, I can help you."

"Yes" said the little mermaid in a trembling voice while thinking of the prince and winning an immortal soul.

"But remember," said the witch, "once you have obtained a human body, you can never again become a mermaid. You will never be able to descend through the waters down to your sisters and to your father's castle. Also, if you do not win the love of the prince, so that for your sake he will forget his father and mother and cling to you with all his thoughts, and let the priest place your hands together so that you become man and wife, then you will not obtain an immortal soul. The morning after he marries someone else your heart will break and you will become foam on the water."

"I want to do it," said the little mermaid, pale as death.

"You also have to pay me," said the witch, "and I demand quite a lot. You have the most lovely voice of anybody at the bottom of the sea, and you probably believe you can charm him with it, but that voice you will have to give me. The best you own I want in exchange for my costly potion. For I have to add my own blood to it that the potion may become as sharp as a two-edged sword."

"But when you take my voice," said the little mermaid, "what do I have left?"

"Your lovely body," said the witch, "your graceful walk and your eloquent eyes. With them you can surely captivate a human heart. Well, have you lost courage? Stick out your tongue, so I may cut it off as payment and I will give you the powerful potion."

"Let it happen," said the little mermaid, and the witch put on the cauldron in order to boil the magic potion. "Cleanliness is a good thing," she said and scrubbed the cauldron with the snakes she had tied into a knot; then she pricked herself in the breast and let her black blood drip down into it. The steam turned into the most horrible shapes and figures, enough to frighten anybody. Every moment the witch added another ingredient to the cauldron, and when it started boiling, it sounded like the weeping of a crocodile. When finally the potion was ready, it looked like the clearest of water.

"There you are," said the witch and cut out the tongue of the little mermaid. Now she was mute, and would never again sing nor talk.

"If the polyps reach out to grab you when you go back through my forest, just throw a single drop of the potion at them, and their arms will explode into a thousand pieces." But the little mermaid had no need to

This half size replica of the statue of The Little Mermaid sits in Denmarket Square in Solvang, California, as one of the many Danish tourist attractions in Solvang. Photo © by Solvang Conference & Visitors Bureau. Website at http://goo.gl/LWSqK

do that, as the polyps withdrew terrified when they saw the glittering potion which shone in her hand, as if it were a twinkling star. Thus she quickly got through the forest, the bog and the roaring maelstroms.

She could see her father's castle. The lights had been turned off in the large dancing hall. Most likely everyone was asleep. She did not dare go to them now that she was mute and was leaving them forever. It was as if her heart would break in agony. She stole into the garden, took a single flower from each of her sisters' flowerbeds, then blew a thousand finger kisses towards the castle and rose up through the dark blue sea.

The sun had not yet risen when she saw the prince's castle and swam up to sit on the gorgeous marble steps, bathed in the moon's clear and lovely light. The little mermaid drank the magic potion and felt as if a two-edged sword went through her delicate body. She fainted and lay as dead. When the sun rose and cast its light over the sea she awoke and felt a burning pain; but right in front of her stood the lovely young prince. He looked at her so earnestly with his jet-black eyes that she lowered her eyes and noticed that her fish tail

Original Illustration by Vilhelm Petersen, 1849

had disappeared and that she had the prettiest little white legs and feet any little girl could have. She was quite naked however, so she swept her long luscious hair around her. The prince asked who she was and how she had come there, and she looked at him with her sad and gentle dark blue eyes. She could not speak. He took her hand and led her into the castle. Every step she took felt as if she stepped on needles and sharp knives, but she suffered it gladly. Holding hands with the prince she moved as light as a bubble and he and everybody else looked in awe at her lovely and graceful movements.

She was dressed in costly garments of silk and muslin. She was the most beautiful girl in the castle, but she was mute and could neither speak nor sing. There were pretty dancing girls, clad in silk and gold who came forward and sang for the prince and his royal parents. One of them sang more beautifully than all the others, and the prince clapped his hands and smiled at her. The little mermaid became sad at this, knowing that she used to have a much lovelier voice, and she thought: "If only he knew that I gave away my voice to be with him for all eternity."

When next the dancing girls danced in lovely, gliding movements to the greatest of music, the little mermaid raised her beautiful white arms, rose on tiptoe and floated over the floor. She danced as no one else had danced. Every movement revealed more of her beauty, and her eyes spoke more eloquently than any song by the dancing girls.

All were enchanted, especially the prince who called her his little foundling. She continued dancing although it was as if she stepped on sharp knives every time her feet touched the ground. The prince said that she should stay with him forever. Henceforth she was allowed to sleep on a cushion of velvet outside his door.

The prince had a page's dress made for her so that she could accompany him on horseback. They rode through the fragrant forests where the green branches touched her shoulders and the little birds sang behind the fresh leaves. Together they climbed the tall mountains and though her feet bled enough to leave prints on the ground, she just laughed and followed him up so high that they saw the clouds sail past beneath them like a flock of birds on their way to foreign lands.

At night in the castle while others slept, she would walk down the wide marble staircase to cool her burning feet in the cold ocean water, and think about all those she knew down in the deep sea.

One night her sisters came, arm in arm. Their song expressed so much grief as they rose above the surface of the water. She waved at them and they recognized her and told her how sad she had made them all. After that evening they visited her every night. One evening far out at sea she saw the old grandmother who for many years had not been to the ocean surface. She also saw her father, the Sea King, with his crown on his head. They stretched their hands towards her, but they did not dare come as close to land as the sisters.

Every day she became dearer to the prince. He loved her as one loves a little dear child, but it never occurred to him to make her his wife. Yet, unless she became his wife she would never obtain an immortal soul and would turn to foam on the sea the morning after his wedding to another.

When he took her into his arms and kissed her lovely forehead her eyes seemed to ask him: "Do you not love me more than all the others?"

"Yes, you are my dearest," said the prince, "for you have the best heart of them all, you are most devoted to me, and you look like a young girl I once saw, but may never find. I once was on a ship which stranded. The waves pushed me onto the shore near a holy temple where several girls were serving. The youngest found me on the beach and saved my life. I only saw her twice, but she was the only one I could love in the whole world. You look like her, and you almost erase her picture in my soul. She belongs to the holy temple, and therefore providence has sent you to me and we will never be parted."

"Oh, he does not know that it was I who saved his life," thought the little mermaid, "I carried him across the sea to the forest where the temple stands. I hid behind rocks and foam to watch over him till someone would find him, and I saw the lovely girl that he loves more than me." And the mermaid drew a deep sigh, as weep she could not. "He says the girl belongs to the holy temple and will never come out

A 1/2 size replica of the statue of The Little Mermaid, in Charlotte Amalie on the island of St. Thomas in the Virgin Islands. The statue is one of the many reminders of the Virgin Islands being Danish for 250 years. Website at http://goo.gl/QTPca

into the world. They will not meet again. I am with him, I see him every day and I will take care of him, love him, and devote my life to him."

But soon it was said that the prince must marry, that the neighboring king's lovely daughter would be his bride, and that a gorgeous ship was being fitted for this purpose. Although the prince gave out that he intended to visit neighboring countries, many thought he was really going to visit the daughter of the king. He planned to bring a large entourage. The little mermaid shook her head and laughed. She knew better than anybody what the prince was really thinking. "I have to go," he had told her, "I must see the beautiful princess. My parents demand it, but they will not force me to bring her back as my bride. I cannot love her, as she will not resemble the beautiful girl in the temple who you look like. Should I ever choose a bride, I would rather it be you, my mute foundling with the eloquent eyes!" and he kissed her red mouth, played with her long hair and laid his head close to her heart, while she dreamt of human happiness and an immortal soul.

"You are not afraid of the sea, my silent child!" he said, when they stood on the beautiful ship that was to take him to the country of the neighboring king. And he told her about storms and calm seas, about strange fish in the deep and what the divers had to tell. And she smiled while listening, for she knew better than anyone about the wonders at the bottom of the sea.

One moonlit night when everybody was asleep, excepting only the first mate who was at the helm, she sat on the railing of the ship and looked down through the clear water, and imagined seeing her father's castle. At the top of the tower her old grandmother stood with the silver crown on her head, staring up through the fast currents towards the keel of the ship. Then her sisters emerged above the waves and looked at her, full of sorrow while wringing their white hands. She waved at them, smiled and wanted to tell them that she was well and happy. But just then the ship's cabin-boy approached, and her sisters dove down so quickly he believed that what he had seen was just white foam on the sea.

The next morning the ship sailed into the neighboring king's magnificent harbor. The church bells were chiming all over town, and trumpets were blown from the tall towers, while soldiers stood with flying colors and shining bayonets. Every day was a feast. Balls and parties were given, one after another. Only the princess was not in attendance. She had not yet arrived. She was being trained in a faraway holy temple, it was said. That was where she was learning royal graces. Then at last the day came when she arrived.

The little mermaid stood waiting to see her beauty, and she had to admit that a lovelier figure she had never seen. Her skin was so delicate and fine and behind the long dark lashes a pair of dark blue, faithful eyes were smiling.

"It is you!" said the prince, "You who saved me when I was lying as dead on the beach!" and he took his blushing bride into his arms. "Oh, I am just too happy!" he said to the little mermaid. "That which I never dared hope has come to pass. You will share my joy, for you love me more than anybody else!" And the little mermaid kissed his hand, and she almost felt her heart break. The morning after his wedding would bring her death and she would dissolve into foam on the sea. All the church bells were ringing and heralds rode through the streets announcing the betrothal. On every altar, fragrant oils were burning in costly silver lamps and priests swung censers with incense. The bride and bridegroom gave each other their hands and received the bishop's blessing. The little mermaid was dressed in silk and gold and held the bride's train, but her ears did not hear the festive music, nor her eyes see the holy ceremony; for she thought only about the night that would mean her death, and about all that she had lost in this world.

When evening came the bride and bridegroom boarded the ship. Cannons roared and all flags were flying. In the middle of the main deck was raised a royal tent covered in gold and crimson cloth. On lovely soft couches and pillows the bridal couple would sleep there through the night. The sails swelled in the wind, and the ship sailed calmly away over the clear sea.

As darkness came the colored lamps were lit and the sailors danced merrily on the deck. The little mermaid could not help recalling the first time she emerged from the sea and saw the same splendor and joy. And she whirled herself into the dance, glided as the swallow glides

This local version of The Little Mermaid in Greenville, Michigan was created by local artist David Willison. The statue is situated on Flat River and is a little more than half the size of the Little Mermaid statue in Copenhagen. Photos © by Darrin Clark.

when he pursues his prey, and everybody cheered her and admired her. Never before had she danced so beautifully. It was as if sharp knives cut through her fine feet, but she did not heed it. There was a sharper pain in her heart. She knew it was the last evening she would see him for whom she had left her family and her home, given away her lovely voice and daily suffered unspeakable pain. And he knew it not. It was the last evening she would breathe the same air as he did, see the deep ocean and the starlit sky. An eternal night without thoughts and dreams awaited her, she who did not have a soul and could not obtain one. All was joy and gaiety on the ship till long past midnight. She laughed and danced with thoughts of death in her heart. The prince kissed his lovely bride, and she played with his dark hair, and embracing each other they went to rest in the gorgeous tent.

Everything became quiet and still on the ship. Only the first mate was at the helm, and the little mermaid put her white arms on the railing and looked eastward for the dawn. She knew that the first ray of sunshine would kill her. Then she caught sight of her sisters emerging from the sea, as pale as she. Their long beautiful hair no longer blew in the wind. It had been cut off.

"We gave it to the sea witch, so she would provide help and not let you die. She has given us a knife, look, here it is, see how sharp it is. Before the sun is up, you must plunge it into the heart of the prince, and when his warm blood splashes onto your feet they will grow together again and form a fish tail. You will become a mermaid again and can come down to us and live out your three hundred years before you die and dissolve into salty foam on the ocean. But hurry up, he or you must die before the sun rises. Our old grandmother's mourning has caused her white hair to fall out as ours fell for the scissors of the witch. Kill the prince and come back. Hurry now. Do you see the red line in the sky? In a few minutes the sun will rise and then you must die." She heard them sigh a strange deep sigh as they sank beneath the waves.

The little mermaid pulled aside the purple cloth of the tent. She saw the lovely bride asleep with her head resting on the chest of the prince. She bent down and kissed his beautiful forehead, then looked at the sky where the dawn became brighter and brighter. She looked at the sharp knife and again looked at the prince who in his dreams mentioned the name of his bride. Only she was in his thoughts. The knife was shaking in the hand of the mermaid – and she threw it far away from her and out into the waves. The water turned red where it fell and it looked like blood oozing out of the waves. Once more she looked longingly at the prince with half glazed eyes, then threw herself into the sea and felt her body dissolving into foam.

The sun rose out of the sea and its rays fell gently and warm on the dead and cold foam, yet the little mermaid did not feel death. She saw the bright sun and up above her flew hundreds of lovely, transparent beings. Through them she could see the white sails on the ship and the red clouds in the sky. Their voices were like music, but so spiritual and ethereal that no human ear could hear it, just as no earthly eye could see them. Without wings they glided by their own lightness through the air. The little mermaid saw that she had a body like theirs which was rising from the foam. "Where am I going?" she asked, and her voice sounded like theirs, more spiritual than any earthly music.

"To the daughters of the air," they answered her. "A mermaid does not have an immortal soul, and can never have one without winning the love of a human. Her eternal existence depends on another being. But while the daughters of the air do not have an eternal soul, they may win one by doing good deeds. We fly to the warm lands where the warm damp air brings illness to people. There we provide coolness. We spread the fragrance of the flowers through the air to bring healing and recuperation. When we have striven to do all the good deeds in our power for three hundred years, we may have an immortal soul and partake in the eternal happiness of human beings. You, poor little mermaid, have tried with all your heart to do the same as we do. You have suffered and endured, and have thereby elevated yourself to the world of the spirits in the air. Now through your continued good deeds you can obtain an immortal soul in three hundred years."

The little mermaid lifted her arms and eyes up towards the sun, and for the first time she felt tears. On the ship there was life and noise again, as the prince and his lovely bride were looking for her. With sadness in their eyes they looked at the bubbling foam as if they knew that she had cast herself into the sea. Unseen she kissed the forehead of the bride, smiled at the prince and then rose with the other daughters of the air up to a rose colored cloud floating in the sky.

Original Illustration by Vilhelm Petersen, 1849

"In three hundred years we will fly into the Kingdom of Heaven," said the little mermaid.

"And we may get there sooner," someone whispered, "Unseen we can enter the houses of men where there are children. Each time we find a good child who is a joy to his parents and deserves their love, our time is shortened. The child does not know when we fly through the room, that we smile with joy at its good conduct, as a year is deducted from the three hundred. But when we see a naughty or wicked child, we shed tears of disappointment, and with each tear a day is added to our time!"

The End

Epilogue

My journey with mermaids started just last year in March 2012, while driving across the United States from Nevada to Cape Cod with my mother.

We stopped on a lark in Elk Horn and Kimballton in Iowa, to see the *Danish Windmill* and the local version of the statue of *The Little Mermaid*.   It was an unplanned stop, but being Danish we couldn't just drive by.

This led to searching the Internet for other copies of *The Little Mermaid* statue, and finding a wealth of mermaid statues all over the world, by hundreds of artists from many diverse cultures, with many different interpretations of mermaids.

It became my passion, and I created the *MermaidsOfEarth.com* website to document and share the many mermaid statues and sculptures, and to promote more mermaid art, in all its forms.

On this website you can find many more photos and much more information on the statues in this book, and many others that have little or nothing in common with *The Little Mermaid*.

Mermaid art can be found almost everywhere, in the form of sculptures and statues, paintings and literature, movies and live performers.

The world of mermaids is one filled with aesthetics and beauty, more than a touch of magic, and all kinds of wonderful people.

It is no wonder that interest in mermaids is a rapidly growing trend.

It is interesting that mermaids are beginning to also be associated strongly with ocean conservation and environmental protection. A number of artists and professional mermaid performers are taking an active role in protecting sealife and habitats, and raising awareness on these issues.

This is visible with initiatives such as *MissionOfMermaids.com* and *SaveTheMermaids.net*, as well as with *HannahMermaid.com*.

I recommend these sites and I wish you a journey through life imbued with beauty and magic.

www.ingramcontent.com/pod-product-compliance
Lightning Source LLC
Chambersburg PA
CBHW041030170626

46815CB00001B/33